187230

PowerKids Readers:

The Bilingual Library of the United States of America™

MINNESOTA

VANESSA BROWN

TRADUCCIÓN AL ESPAÑOL: MARÍA CRISTINA BRUSCA

The Rosen Publishing Group's
PowerKids Press™ & **Editorial Buenas Letras**™
New York

Published in 2006 by The Rosen Publishing Group, Inc.
29 East 21st Street, New York, NY 10010

First Edition

Book Design: Albert B. Hanner
Photo Credits: Cover, p. 11 © Raymond Gehman/Corbis; p. 5 © Joseph Sohm; Chromosohm Inc./Corbis; p. 7 © 2002 Geoatlas; p. © 9 David Muench/Corbis; p. 13 © Corbis; p. 15 © Julie Habe/Corbis; p. 17 © Francis G. Mayer/Corbis; pp. 19, 31 (ice fishing, sled) © Layne Kennedy/Corbis; pp. 21, 30 (state motto, Red or Norway Pine, North Star State, The Gopher State) © Richard Hamilton Smith/Corbis; p. 23 © Owaki - Kulla/Corbis; pp. 25, 30 (capital) © Richard Cummins/Corbis; pp. 30 (Showy Lady Slipper) © Ed Wargin/Corbis; p. 30 © (Loon) © Gunter Marx Photography/Corbis; p. 31 (Little Crow) © Minnesota Historical Society/Corbis; p. 31 (Schultz, Dylan) © Bettmann/Corbis; p. 31 (Mondale) © Roger Ressmeyer/Corbis, p. 31 (Lange) © Douglas Kirkland/Corbis; p. 31 (Scurry) © Duomo/Corbis

Library of Congress Cataloging-in-Publication Data

Brown, Vanessa, 1963–
Minnesota / Vanessa Brown ; traducción al español, María Cristina Brusca.— 1st ed.
p. cm. — (The bilingual library of the United States of America) Includes bibliographical references and index.
ISBN 1-4042-3088-2 (library binding)
1. Minnesota–Juvenile literature. I. Title. II. Series.
F606.3.B76 2006
977.6—dc22
2005010831

Due to the changing nature of Internet links, Editorial Buenas Letras has developed an online list of Web sites related to the subject of this book. This site is updated regularly. Please use this link to access the list:

http://www.buenasletraslinks.com/ls/minnesota

Contents

Contenido

Welcome to Minnesota

These are the flag and seal of the state of Minnesota. The banner on the seal has the state motto written in French. It says *l'etoile du nord*, which means "the star of the north."

Bienvenidos a Minnesota

Estos son la bandera y el escudo del estado de Minnesota. La banda del escudo tiene el lema del estado escrito en francés. El lema dice *l' etoile du nord*, lo que quiere decir "la estrella del norte".

Minnesota Flag and State Seal

Bandera y escudo de Minnesota

Minnesota Geography

Minnesota is located in the north central part of the United States. It borders the states of North Dakota, South Dakota, Iowa, and Wisconsin, and the country of Canada.

Geografía de Minnesota

Minnesota está ubicado en la zona central y norte, de los Estados Unidos. Minnesota linda con los estados de Dakota del Norte, Dakota del Sur, Iowa, Wisconsin y el país de Canadá.

Rainy Lake
Lago Rainy

CANADA
CANADÁ

Lake of the Woods
Lago de los Bosques

Red Lake
Lago Rojo

Hibbing ○

Lake Superior
Lago Superior

Bemidji ○

NORTH DAKOTA
DAKOTA DEL NORTE

Duluth ○

MINNESOTA

Mississippi River
Río Misisipi

SOUTH DAKOTA
DAKOTA DEL SUR

WISCONSIN

Minnesota River
Río Minnesota

Map Key
Claves del mapa

○ Major City
  Ciudad principal

Lake Minnetonka
Lago Minnetonka

Minneapolis ○ ★
         St.Paul

⭐ Capital
  Capital

Des Moines River
Río Des Moines

Rochester ○

～ River
  Río

Fairmont ○

NEBRASKA

Map of Minnesota

Mapa de Minnesota

IOWA

Minnesota is called the Land of 10,000 Lakes. The state borders the largest of the Great Lakes, Lake Superior. The largest lake in the state is Red Lake. Other large lakes are Lake of the Woods, Lake Minnetonka, and Rainy Lake.

Minnesota es conocida como la "Tierra de los 10,000 Lagos". El estado bordea el lago Superior, que es el mayor de los Grandes Lagos. El lago más grande del estado es el lago Rojo. Otros grandes lagos son el lago de los Bosques, lago Minnetonka y lago Rainy.

Split Rock Lighthouse on Lake Superior

Faro Split Rock en el lago Superior

Minnesota has one national park. It is called the Voyageurs. Minnesota also has two national forests. They are Superior National Forest and the Chippewa National Forest.

Minessota tiene un parque nacional, llamado Voyageurs. Minnesota tiene también dos bosques nacionales. Estos son el Bosque Nacional Superior y el Bosque Nacional Chippewa.

Superior National Forest

Bosque Nacional Superior

Minnesota History

Many Native American groups lived in Minnesota. The Dakota were the main group. Others like the Chippewa, the Arapaho, the Cree, and the Fox also lived in the region.

Historia de Minnesota

Varios grupos de nativos americanos vivían en Minnesota. La tribu principal era la de los Dakota. Otros grupos, como los Chippewa, los Arapaho, los Cree y los Fox, también vivían en la región.

A Chippewa Indian Family

Una familia de Indios Chippewa

The name "Minnesota" comes from the Dakota Indian word *mnishota*. It means "cloudy" or "milky water." This describes the light-colored, sandy water of the Minnesota River.

El nombre "Minnesota" viene de *mnishota*, una palabra indígena Dakota, que quiere decir "nublado" o "agua lechosa". Estas palabras describen las aguas arenosas, de colores claros, del río Minnesota.

Sunset on the Minnesota River

Puesta de sol en el río Minnesota

In 1819, the U.S. Army set up Fort Snelling. For more than 30 years this place was a meeting point for fur traders, Native Americans, and soldiers.

En 1819, el ejército de los Estados Unidos estableció el Fuerte Snelling. Durante más de 30 años este lugar fue un punto de encuentro para los comerciantes de pieles, nativos americanos y soldados.

View of Fort Snelling

Vista del Fuerte Snelling

Living in Minnesota

Winters in Minnesota are very cold. The record low temperature is -60° F (-51° C)! Many Minnesotans take advantage of this weather. They enjoy skiing, ice-fishing, and riding snowmobiles and sleds.

La vida en Minnesota

Los inviernos en Minnesota son muy fríos. ¡La temperatura más baja registrada es –60°F (-51°C)! Muchos minesotanos aprovechan este clima, disfrutando del esquí o la pesca en el hielo y paseando en trineo o motonieve.

Ice Fishing on a Frozen Lake in Minnesota

Pescando en el hielo en un lago helado en Minnesota

Minneapolis and St. Paul are known as the twin cities. This cities are separated by the Mississippi River. The Twin Cities area is a great place to see theater and musical events.

Minneapolis y St. Paul Minnesota son conocidas como las ciudades gemelas. Estas dos ciudades están separadas por el río Mississippi. El área de las ciudades gemelas es un buen lugar para asistir a eventos de teatro y música.

View of Minneapolis, One of the Twin Cities

Vista de Minneapolis, una de las ciudades gemelas

The largest shopping mall in the United States is Mall of America in Bloomington, Minnesota. More than 11,000 Minnesotans work in Mall of America, and more than 40 million visit every year.

El centro comercial más grande de los Estados Unidos es el Mall of America y está en Bloomington, Minnesota. Más de 11,000 minesotanos trabajan en el Mall of America y más de 40 millones lo visitan cada año.

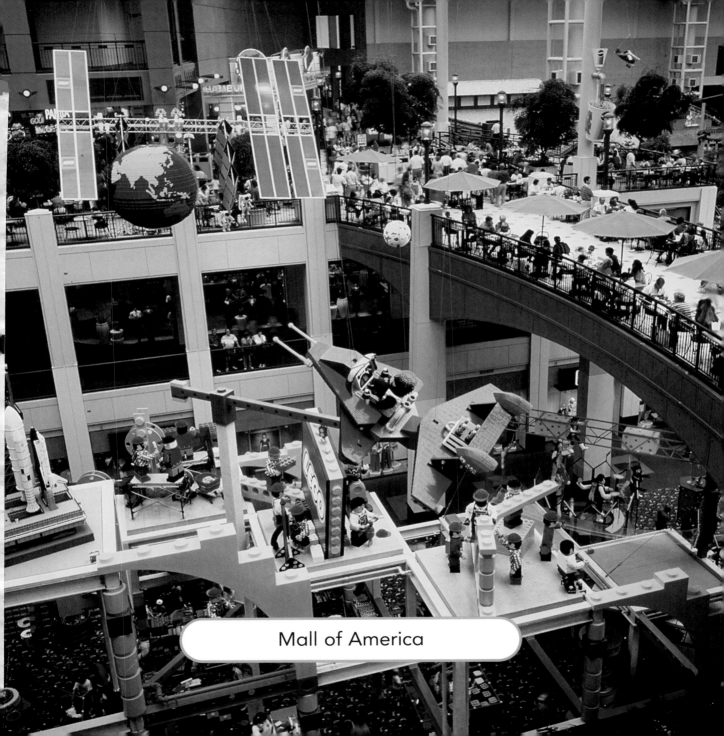

Mall of America

Minneapolis, St. Paul, Duluth, and Rochester are important cities in Minnesota. St. Paul is the capital of the state.

Minneapolis, St. Paul, Duluth y Rochester son ciudades importantes de Minnesota. St. Paul es la capital del estado.

Minnesota State Capitol in St. Paul

Capitolio del estado de Minnesota en St. Paul

Activity:
Let's draw the Map of Minnesota

Actividad:
Dibujemos el mapa de Minnesota

1

Draw a vertical rectangle.

Dibuja un rectángulo vertical.

2

Using the rectangle, draw the outline of the shape of the state.

Usando el rectángulo dibuja la forma exterior del estado.

3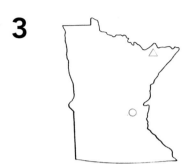

Erase the rectangle guide and draw a circle for Minneapolis. Draw a triangle for Superior National Forest.

Borra el rectángulo de guía y dibuja un círculo en el lugar de Minneapolis. Dibuja un triángulo para marcar el Bosque Nacional Superior.

4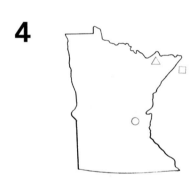

Now draw the square for Lake Superior.

Ahora, traza un cuadrado en el lugar del lago Superior.

5

To finish your map, draw a star to mark Minnesota's capital, St. Paul.

Para terminar, dibuja una estrella para marcar St. Paul, la capital de Minnesota.

Timeline		Cronología
French traders Radisson and Groseilliers reach Lake Superior.	**1656**	Los comerciantes franceses Radisson y Groseilliers llegan al lago Superior.
President Thomas Jefferson buys western Minnesota in the Louisiana Purchase.	**1803**	El presidente Thomas Jefferson compra la zona oeste de Minnesota en la Compra de Luisiana.
The U.S. Army set up Fort Snelling.	**1819**	El ejército de E.U.A. establece el Fuerte Snelling.
Minnesota becomes the thirty-second state of the Union.	**1858**	Minnesota se convierte en el estado número treintaidós de la Unión.
Minnesota's third and present capitol building is completed.	**1905**	Se completa el tercer y actual capitolio del estado.
The American Indian Movement (AIM) is founded in Minneapolis to combat racism.	**1968**	El Movimiento Nativoamericano es fundado en Minneapolis para combatir el racismo.
The Minnesota Twins baseball team win their first World Series.	**1987**	El equipo de béisbol de los Minnesota Twins gana su primera Serie Mundial.

Minnesota Events	Eventos en Minnesota

January
Saint Paul Winter Carnival

April
The Festival of Nations
in Minneapolis
Minneapolis/St. Paul International
Film Festival

May
Cinco de Mayo celebrations in
Minneapolis and St. Paul

June
Minnesota Folk Festival
in Hastings

July
Northwest Water Carnival
in Detroit Lakes
Minneapolis Aquatennial

August
Annual Pine to Palm Golf Tournament
in Detroit Lakes
Minnesota State Fair in St. Paul

December
AIM powwow at Fort Snelling

Enero
Carnaval de invierno de Saint Paul

Abril
El festival de las naciones, en
Minneapolis
Festival internacional de cine de
Minneapolis y St. Paul

Mayo
Celebraciones del Cinco de Mayo en
Minneapolis y St. Paul

Junio
Festival folclórico de Minnesota, en
Hastings

Julio
Carnaval acuático del noroeste, en Detroit
Lakes
Festival acuático de Minneapolis

Agosto
Torneo anual de golf Pine to Palm, en
Detroit Lakes
Feria del estado de Minnesota

Diciembre
Powow AIM, en Fort Snelling

Minnesota Facts/Datos sobre Minnesota

Population
4.9 million

Población
4.9 millones

Capital
St. Paul

Capital
St. Paul

State Motto
L'etoile du nord,
Star of the North.

Lema del estado
L'etoile du nord,
La estrella del norte

State Flower
Showy Lady Slipper
(Cypripedium reginae)

Flor del estado
Orquídea Cypripedium
reginae

State Bird
Loon

Ave del estado
Somorgujo

State Nickname
North Star State, The
Gopher State

Mote del estado
Estado de la Estrella del
Norte, Estado de la ardilla
terrera

State Tree
Red or Norway Pine

Árbol del estado
Pino rojo o de Noruega

State Song
"Hail, Minnesota"

Canción del estado
"Saludo a Minnesota"

30

Famous Minnesotans/Minesotanos famosos

Little Crow Ta-oyate-duta *(1810–1863)*

Indian leader

Líder nativoamericano

Charles M. Schulz *(1922–2002)*

Cartoonist

Autor de cómics

Walter Mondale *(1928–   )*

U.S. vice president

Vicepresidente de los E.U.A.

Bob Dylan *(1941–   )*

Singer/songwriter

Cantautor

Jessica Lange *(1949–   )*

Actress

Actriz

Briana Scurry *(1971–   )*

Soccer player

Jugadora de fútbol

Words to Know/Palabras que debes saber

banner

banda

border

frontera

ice-fishing

pesca en hielo

sled

trineo

Here are more books to read about Minnesota:

Otros libros que puedes leer sobre Minnesota:

In English/En inglés:

Minnesota
Hello USA
by Porter, A. P.
Lerner Publications, 2001

Minnesota: Land of 10,000 Lakes
World Almanac Library of the States
by Pollock, Miriam Heddy, Jaffe, Peter
Gareth Stevens Publishing, 2002

Words in English: 321

Palabras en español: 363

Index

Índice